The Childhood of Ambedkar

MAHESH DUTT SHARMA

Published by
PRABHAT PRAKASHAN PVT. LTD.
4/19 Asaf Ali Road,
New Delhi-110 002 (INDIA)
e-mail: prabhatbooks@gmail.com

ISBN 978-93-5562-930-2
THE CHILDHOOD OF AMBEDKAR
by Mahesh Dutt Sharma

Edition
First, 2024

Price
₹ 250 (Rupees Two Hundred Fifty Only)

Printed at
Sita Fine Arts, Delhi

Author's Note

Babasaheb B.R. Ambedkar is known as the chief architect of the Indian Constitution and a vocal spokesperson for Dalit rights. He was born into an untouchable caste known as 'Mahar' - a group viewed as 'our village servants' by the British. He experienced discrimination from an early age, which he described clearly in his later writings. At one place he writes-

"While in school, I knew that when children from the general category were thirsty, they could go to a water tap, open it and quench their thirst, but my situation was different. I could not touch the tap and it was not possible to quench my thirst unless any common man opened the tap for me."

Despite his low caste, Ambedkar's father became an officer in the Indian Army and placed special emphasis on the education of his children. At that time, teachers were often reluctant to educate Dalit children. They often refused to take their examination.

Ambedkar was the first person in his community to graduate. He did his Bachelor of Arts in Economics and Political Science from the University of Bombay. Here, he met Maharaja Sayajirao III of the princely state of Baroda.

The Maharaja was an active advocate of social reforms including the eradication of untouchability. He sent Ambedkar abroad for further education, first to Columbia University in New York where he completed his Masters and Ph.D. and later, to the London School of Economics and Political Science.

During this period, Ambedkar studied Economics, History and Political Science and wrote on a wide range of subjects, including the history of caste in India.

Ambedkar's studies were interrupted by the war and the termination of his scholarship in 1917. He was obliged to return to India, where he was forcibly reminded of his untouchable status, something he had forgotten while studying in the West. Even when he was appointed at Sydenham College of Commerce and Economics in Bombay as professor in 1995, other faculty members objected to his use of water jugs.

This was the time when he started campaigning for Dalit rights. In 1920, he started a weekly Marathi newspaper, which strongly criticised caste discrimination and called for Dalit awakening and mobilisation against inequality.

Later, with the financial support of the Maharaja of Kolhapur, he went to London to complete his studies and on his return to Bombay in 1924, founded the 'Bahishkrit Hitkarini Sabha' (Group for the Welfare of the Excluded) to promote socio-political awareness among the Dalits and raise public awareness about their grievances and intensified his campaign for social reform.

In the next twenty years, he played an important role in organising the untouchables. He founded Dalit newspapers as well as social and cultural institutions, participated in conferences of the Dalit classes, initiated protests against discrimination in temple entry and access to water and promoted Dalit access to education.

At the same time, he took advantage of the opportunities offered by the British government to petition for political rights, even on occasions when the Indian National Congress chose to boycott constitutional reform discussions, such as during the Simon Commission. He founded two political parties to contest elections awarded by the British in 1937 and 1946, although these had little success against the resource-rich Congress Party.

Although he was critical of the British colonial government, Ambedkar often sided with the Congress and the nationalist movement, as he primarily struggled to address the issue of untouchability. In 1932, the British Prime Minister, Ramsay MacDonald, offered the Communal Award to provide separate electorates for minorities, including the untouchables, but Gandhi was adamant that he could not accept such a split in the Hindu vote and started a fast unto death, forcing Ambedkar to retreat and agree to a joint electorate.

Relations between the two deteriorated rapidly during the 1930s. Instead of rejecting the caste system, Ambedkar saw Gandhi's efforts to persuade Hindus to reform as ineffective and an obstacle to Dalit political rights. In the latter half of the 1930s, Gandhi and Ambedkar corresponded briefly, highlighting their differences and in the 1940s, Ambedkar wrote two treatises, criticising the Congress and Gandhi and accusing them of gross hypocrisy.

Despite Ambedkar's differences with the Congress, when India became independent in August 1947, Prime Minister Nehru invited him to become the first Minister of Law and Justice. Shortly afterwards, the Constituent Assembly appointed Ambedkar as the Chairman of the Drafting Committee for the new Constitution.

Ambedkar's influence can be seen in many aspects of the resulting Indian Constitution, such as the emphasis on liberal democracy and federal structure, provisions and safeguards for minorities as well as the vigorous abolition of untouchability.

The Constitution was promulgated on 26 January 1950. Ambedkar appreciated that it had its limits and declared that political democracy could have no meaning without social democracy. The Congress refused to agree to a uniform civil code that would have been socially progressive, such as in advancing gender equality; but it would have restricted the ability of Hindus and Muslims to follow personal religious laws. This led Ambedkar to resign from his post as Minister of Law and Justice in 1951.

However, he was confident that the new Constitution represented a solid foundation for the creation of India as a new independent nation—"I think the Constitution is practical; it is flexible and strong enough to keep the country together, both in times of peace and in times of war. In fact, if I may say so, if things go wrong under the new Constitution, it will not be because our Constitution was bad. What we have to say is that man was corrupt."

The heart-touching story of Babasaheb B.R. Ambedkar's endless struggle, in which, his childhood struggle has been vocally expressed.

❑

Contents

1

Success Through Struggle

"Mahatmas came and went, but untouchables remain untouchables."

–Bhimrao Ambedkar

Born in Madhya Pradesh, Bhimrao Ambedkar was an Indian jurist, statesman, philosopher, thinker, anthropologist, historian, orator, prolific writer, economist, scholar, editor, revolutionary and revivalist of Buddhism in India. He was the chief architect of the Indian Constitution. His struggle for the dignity and rights of the untouchables/Dalits was an exemplary event in the history of human rights of India. Ambedkar spent his entire life fighting against social discrimination, the system of Chaturvarna—the Hindu classification of human society into four varnas—and the caste system. Dr. Ambedkar's efforts to eradicate social evils like untouchability and caste restrictions were remarkable. The leader fought for the rights of Dalits and other socially backward classes throughout his life. He was appointed as the country's first Law Minister in the cabinet of Jawaharlal Nehru. He is credited with giving birth to a bloodless revolution with his most notable and innovative movement of liberty, equality and fraternity for the upliftment of the Dalit masses, guided by the Buddhist philosophy of liberty, equality and fraternity. He was posthumously awarded India's highest civilian award, the 'Bharat Ratna', in 1990.

Life Sketch

Bhimrao Ramji Ambedkar was born on 14 April 1891 in Madhya Pradesh to Bhimabai and Ramji Sakpal. He was the fourteenth child of his parents. Ambedkar's father was a Subedar in the Indian army and posted in Mhow Cantonment in Madhya Pradesh. After his father's retirement in 1894, the his family moved to Satara, a small town in Maharashtra. His mother died shortly afterwards, his father remarried and the family relocated to Bombay, where he qualified for his matriculation in 1908. Bhimrao

Ambedkar was a victim of caste discrimination. His parents belonged to the Hindu Mahar caste, which was viewed as 'untouchable' by the prevailing Hindu social system.

Bhimrao Ramji Ambedkar was born on 14 April 1891 in Madhya Pradesh to Bhimabai and Ramji Sakpal. He was the fourteenth child of his parents. Ambedkar's father was a Subedar in the Indian army and posted in Mhow Cantonment in Madhya Pradesh.

Bhimrao Ambedkar had to face serious discrimination in everyday life from every corner of the society. This discrimination and humiliation troubled Ambedkar even in the Army School run by the British Government. Fearing social resentment, teachers would separate lower caste students from Brahmins and other upper castes. Teachers often asked untouchable students to sit outside the classroom.

After shifting to Satara, he was enrolled in a local school, but changing schools did not change the fate of young Bhimrao; he became a victim of discrimination wherever he went. In 1908, Ambedkar got the opportunity to study at Elphinstone College, Mumbai to pursue his Bachelor of Arts. As he was an intelligent student, he had been awarded a scholarship of Rs.25/- per month by

Sayajirao III, the Gaekwad ruler of the contemporaneous state of Baroda. He graduated from Bombay University in Political Science and Economics in 1912.

Bhimrao Ambedkar had to face serious discrimination in everyday life from every corner of the society. This discrimination and humiliation troubled Ambedkar even in the Army School run by the British Government.

He went to Columbia University, USA for his higher studies. He was awarded his doctorate on 8 June 1927. In November 2011, the same university, on the completion of its 300th year, shortlisted six era-building individuals, among whom Dr. B.R. Ambedkar was recognised as an icon and honoured by placing his bronze statue at the main entrance of the university. He was called a symbol of knowledge and the plaque reads – 'Salute to Dr. Ambedkar'.

After returning from the United States, Dr. Ambedkar was appointed as the Defence Secretary to the king of Baroda, but he had to face humiliation on account of being 'untouchable'. The subordinates in the office were not ready to sit with him. Even the peons would throw and take away files from a distance.

With the help of Lord Sydenham, former Governor of Bombay, Ambedkar obtained a job as Professor of Political

Economy at the Sydenham College of Commerce and Economics in Bombay. He went to England in 1920 to pursue his further studies and was awarded a D.Sc. degree by the University of London. He also spent a few months studying Economics at the University of Bonn in Germany.

After returning from the United States, Dr. Ambedkar was appointed as the Defence Secretary to the King of Baroda, but he had to face humiliation on account of being 'untouchable'.

Social Reform Movement

Being an untouchable, Dr. Ambedkar had to face humiliation and he even had to face abuse by his subordinates. The strangest situation was when he did not tell his caste to the caretaker of the Parsi lodge. After his identity was known, he was thrown out of the lodge. It pained him like an open wound. This incident made him realise that being educated in the best universities of the world cannot uplift his status and it is similar to that of millions of illiterate people who suffer discrimination and exploitation.

Bhimrao Ambedkar decided to fight against caste discrimination which had almost torn the nation apart. He started finding ways to reach out to the people and make them understand the shortcomings of the prevalent social evils. He launched a newspaper named 'Mooknayak' (Leader of the Dumb) and wrote vociferously on the atrocities of the caste system and its forms of exploitation. It is said that one day, after hearing his speech at a rally, Chhatrapati Shahu IV, an influential ruler of Kolhapur, dined with the leader. This incident created uproar in the socio-political sphere of the country, even among those who had supported his higher education abroad by giving him some fellowships.

Bhimrao Ambedkar decided to fight against caste discrimination, which had almost torn the nation apart. He started finding ways to reach out to the people and make them understand the shortcomings of the prevalent social evils.

His reform movements for entry into temples and protest against untouchability towards water were milestones in the history of social upheaval in India. For Dalits and Ambedkarites in India, 25 December is remembered as 'Manusmriti' burning day, the day B.R. Ambedkar publicly and formally burnt the 'Manusmriti' in 1927. On July 8, 1945, he started the historic People's Education Society and a Law College in Wadala, Mumbai to introduce education as the foundation of the social movement in Aurangabad, Maharashtra.

Political Philosophy and Career

His political philosophy was linked to the social philosophy of Buddha. On the principle of democracy he said, "What we must do is not to content ourselves with only political democracy. We should also make our political democracy, a social democracy. Political democracy cannot survive unless there is social democracy at its base. What does social democracy mean? It means a way of life which recognises liberty, equality and fraternity as principles of life. These principles of liberty, equality and fraternity should not be considered as separate items. They form a union in the sense that to divorce one from the other is to defeat the very purpose of democracy. Liberty cannot be separated from equality, nor can liberty and equality be separated from fraternity."

What we must do is not to content ourselves with only political democracy. We should also make our political democracy, a social democracy. Political democracy cannot survive unless there is social democracy at its base.

In the claim of his social philosophy, he attests to the source of his strength, "In a positive way, my social philosophy can be summed up in three words – liberty, equality and fraternity. Even then, if someone says that I have borrowed my philosophy from the French revolution, no. The roots of my philosophy are in religion and not in political science. I have received them from the teachings of my Guru Buddha."

In 1936, Dr. Ambedkar formed an Independent Labour Party and his party won 15 seats in the 1937 Central Assembly Elections. The party had been changed into the All India Scheduled Castes Federation, but performed poorly in the 1946 elections for the Constituent Assembly of India. Dr. Ambedkar objected to the decision of the Congress and Mahatma Gandhi to call the untouchable community, Harijan. When Ramsay Macdonald announced the Communal Award, Mahatma Gandhi went on a fast unto death, primarily because Dr. Ambedkar was of the opinion that there should be a separate electoral system for untouchables and lower caste people. Dr. Ambedkar compromised to save the life of Barrister Mahatma Gandhi, as this had increased tensions outside(?) the country. He also supported the concept of providing reservations for Dalits and other marginalised communities. He said that the members of the untouchable community are also like other members of the society. Dr. Ambedkar was appointed as the Labour Minister in the Defence Advisory Committee and the Viceroy's Executive Council. During his tenure, he continuously raised his voice to protect the interests of the working classes. Chief Architect of the Indian Constitution

Just after independence, Dr. Ambedkar was appointed the Chairman of the Constitution Drafting Committee. He was an eminent scholar and also a renowned jurist. He emphasised on building a virtual bridge between different sections of the society. According to him, it would be difficult to maintain the unity of the country if the differences between classes and castes were not bridged. As a strong advocate of human rights for the society in general and the depressed classes in particular, he said, "The problem of Dalits is not poverty alone, but lack of basic human rights."

While presenting the Constitution, he had many apprehensions on the dual nature of Indian society and its politics. He said, "On 26 January 1950, we are going to enter a life of contradictions. In politics, we will have equality and in social and economic life, we will have inequality. In politics, we will recognise the principle of one person one vote and one vote one value. In our social and economic life, because of our social and economic structure, we will continue to deny the principle of one person one value. How

Just after independence, Dr. Ambedkar was appointed the Chairman of the Constitution Drafting Committee. He was an eminent scholar and also a renowned jurist. He emphasised on building a virtual bridge between different sections of the society.

long will we continue to live this life of contradictions? How long will we continue to deny equality in our social and economic lives? If we continue to deny it for much longer, we will only do so by endangering our political democracy. We must resolve this contradiction as soon as possible; otherwise, those who suffer from inequality will destroy the structure of democracy that this Constituent Assembly has worked so hard to build."

First Law Minister

He was appointed as the first Law Minister of independent India and Chairman of the committee responsible for drafting the Constitution. He was trying his best to ensure equality among the masses and was against the ill-treatment of women and the marginalised sections of the society, because traditions like sati, destitution and untouchability were prevalent in Hindu society. He drafted a motion in Parliament aimed at conservative Hindus and the reform of the caste system and named it as the Hindu Code Bill. It aimed to bring gender equality in the laws of inheritance and marriage, but was not passed, mainly

> *He was appointed as the first Law Minister of independent India and Chairman of the committee responsible for drafting the Constitution. He was trying his best to ensure equality among the masses.*

because of the dominance of members who supported patriarchy. Therefore, he resigned from the Nehru cabinet in protest in 1951.

Leading Economic Planner

Ambedkar was the first Indian to do a doctorate in Economics abroad. He had a broad understanding of the social and economic deprivation in society based on inequality, so he stressed that industrialisation and agricultural development can boost the Indian economy. He emphasised on investment in agriculture as India's primary industry. According to many scholars, Dr. Ambedkar's vision has and will continue to guide governments to achieve the goal of food security. Ambedkar advocated national, economic and social development with emphasis on education, public sanitation, community health and residential facilities as basic amenities. His D.Sc. thesis, 'Problems of the Rupee, Its Origin and Solutions' (1923), examines the reasons for the decline in the value of the rupee. He proved the importance of price stability over exchange stability. He analysed the exchange rates of silver and gold and their effect on the economy. He explored the reasons for the failure of the public treasury of British India and calculated the loss of development caused by British rule.

Ambedkar was the first Indian to do a doctorate in Economics abroad. He had a broad understanding of the social and economic deprivation in society based on inequality, so he stressed that industrialisation and agricultural development can boost the Indian economy. He emphasised on investment in agriculture as India's primary industry.

Historically, Dr. Ambedkar established the Finance Commission of India in 1951. He opposed income tax for low-income groups in order to rationalise income and taxation. He contributed to land revenue tax and excise policies to stabilise the economy. He played an important role in land reforms and the economic development of the state. According to him, the caste system, rather than the division of labour, divided labourers and hindered economic progress. He was perhaps the only scholar who distinguished between surplus labour and ideal labour. He emphasised on a free economy with a stable rupee, which India had recently adopted. He advocated birth control to develop the Indian economy and it was adopted by the Government of India as a national policy for family planning. He emphasised on equal rights of women for economic development. He laid the foundation of industrial relations after Indian independence.

Dr. Ambedkar's philosophical guide, John Dewey once said – "Every society is burdened with trifles, with the deadwood of the past and with things positively distorted. As a society becomes more enlightened, it realises that it is not responsible for preserving and disseminating its entire achievement, but only for aiming at a better society."

Historically, Dr. Ambedkar established the Finance Commission of India in 1951. He opposed income tax for low-income groups in order to rationalise income and taxation. He contributed to land revenue tax and excise policies to stabilise the economy.

But it appears that Dr. Ambedkar wanted to convert his idea into reality with his reformist approach and for which, he struggled throughout his life.

Contribution in the Formation of the Reserve Bank of India

Before his entry into politics, he was a professional economist till 1921. He wrote three books on Economics which reveal the administrative and financial nature of the colonial British and also emphasise on necessary measures to develop and strengthen financial structures. These books are –

- Administration and Finance of the East India Company,

- Development of Provincial Finance in British India,
- The Rupee Problem: Its Origin and its Solution.

In fact, the Reserve Bank of India (RBI) was formed on the basis of the ideas that Dr. Ambedkar had presented to the Hilton Young commission during the pre- independence period.

Before his entry into politics, he was a professional economist till 1921. He wrote three books on Economics which reveal the administrative and financial nature of the colonial British India and also emphasise on necessary measures to develop and strengthen financial structures.

Adopting Buddhism

Despite having the option of joining Sikhism, Islam and Christianity, he preferred the indigenous path of Buddha and his Dhamma. After the Poona Pact and other reform movements in 1932, he gained extensive experience on the straitjacket of the Hindu social order and plight of the untouchables.

In a meeting, he clarified the concept of religion and said, "I tell you that religion is for man; man is not for religion. If you want to be organised, integrated and successful in this world, change this religion. A religion that does not recognise you as a human being or does not give you water to drink or does not allow you to enter temples does not deserve to be called a religion. A religion that stops you from gaining education and hinders your material progress does not deserve the position of a 'religion'. A religion that does not teach its followers to show humanity in dealing with their co-religionists is nothing but a display of power. A religion which teaches its followers to tolerate the touch of animals but not the touch of humans is not a religion, but a joke. A religion which forces the ignorant to remain ignorant and the poor to remain poor is not religion but philosophy. The basic idea of religion is to create an environment for the spiritual development of an individual. It is clear that you cannot develop your personality at all in the Hindu religion."

In a meeting, he clarified the concept of religion and said, "I tell you that religion is for man; man is not for religion. If you want to be organised, integrated and successful in this world, change this religion."

At a Mahar conference in Yeola, Maharashtra, in 1935 he said, "I am born a Hindu, which was not in my hands but I will not die a Hindu."

In 1950, Ambedkar went to Sri Lanka to participate in a conference of Buddhist scholars and monks. On his return, he decided to write a book on Buddhism and soon converted to Buddhism. He criticised Hindu customs and caste division in his speeches. He said, "There is no room for development in conscience, logic and free thinking in Hinduism. Your claim of equality hurts them. They want to maintain the status quo. If you continue to accept your lowly position without any hesitation, remaining dirty, backward, ignorant, poor and uncultured, they will let you live in peace. The moment you start raising your level, the struggle begins. Untouchability is not a transitory or temporary characteristic; it is eternal. It can be clearly said that the struggle between Hindus and untouchables is a never-ending one. It is eternal, because a religion that grants you the lowest status in society is itself divine and eternal as per the belief of the so-called upper caste Hindus. Any change expected due to change in time and circumstances is not possible."

On 14 October 1956, Ambedkar organised a public event to convert about five lakh of his supporters to Buddhism. He gave 22 vows to his followers present in Nagpur and urged to practice them in their lives. This place later came to be known as 'Diksha Bhoomi'. Ambedkar travelled to Kathmandu to participate in the Fourth World Buddhist Conference. He completed his final manuscript, 'The

In 1950, Ambedkar went to Sri Lanka to participate in a conference of Buddhist scholars and monks. On his return, he decided to write a book on Buddhism and soon converted to Buddhism.

Buddha or Karl Marx' on 2 December, 1956. His book, 'The Buddha and His Dhamma' was published posthumously.

In fact, his interpretation of Buddha and his Dhamma was qualitatively different from that of other Brahmin and oriental scholars. Dr. Ambedkar was the founder of the Indian Buddhist Mahasabha as a cultural organisation. Thus, he was not only critical but experimental in solving problems and creating revolution and as such, his achievements were remarkable. Thus, he was established as a revivalist.

On 14 October 1956, Ambedkar organised a public event to convert about five lakh of his supporters to Buddhism. He gave 22 vows to his followers present in Nagpur and urged to practice them in their lives. This place later came to be known as 'Diksha Bhoomi'.

Demise

During 1954-55, Dr. Ambedkar suffered from serious health issues including diabetes and poor eyesight, but was still keen to complete his two important books, 'Buddha or Karl Marx' and 'Buddha and his Dhamma'. He died on 6 December 1956 at his residence on Alipore Road in Delhi. Since Dr. Ambedkar had adopted Buddhism as his religion, a Buddhist-cultural cremation was organised for him. The ceremony was attended by thousands of his supporters, workers and admirers at Juhu beach, Mumbai, which is known as 'Chaitya Bhoomi'. Every year on 6 December, lakhs of his followers pay their respects to the great leader, Dr. Ambedkar.

❑

2

A Living Legacy

"Some people think that there is no need of religion for society, but I do not agree with this idea. The establishment of religion is extremely important for human life."

–Bhimrao Ambedkar

The legacy of Dr. Ambedkar, as a man of many talents and a socio-political reformist, had a deep impact on independent and modern India. His socio-political views are respected across the political spectrum in post-independence India. His initiatives have impacted various walks of life and changed the way India looks at socio-economic policies, education and affirmative action today, through socio-economic and legal incentives. He passionately believed in individual freedom and criticised the caste society. His accusations regarding Hinduism as the foundation of the caste system made him unpopular and controversial among the Hindus, but all his concepts and convictions were clear and well-reasoned. His conversion to Buddhism led to a revival of interest in Buddhist philosophy in India and abroad.

Several public institutions have been named in his honour. A large official portrait of Dr. Ambedkar is displayed in the Indian Parliament. Dr. Ambedkar was chosen as 'Greatest Indian' in a survey conducted by History TV-18 and CNN-IBN in 2012. Nearly 20 million votes were cast, making him the most popular Indian person since the launch of the initiative.

Several public institutions have been named in his honour. A large official portrait of Dr. Ambedkar is displayed in the Indian Parliament. Dr. Ambedkar was chosen as 'Greatest Indian' in a survey conducted by History TV-18 and CNN-IBN in 2012. Nearly 20 million votes were cast, making him the most popular Indian person since the launch of the initiative.

Because of his role in Economics, Dr. Narendra Jadhav, a noted Indian economist, has said that Ambedkar was the "greatest economist of all time". The great award-winning Professor Amartya Sen said that "Ambedkar is my father of Economics. His contribution to the field of Economics is amazing and will always be remembered." Osho, a spiritual teacher, commented, "I have seen people who were born in the lowest category of Hindu law – Shudra, untouchable, so intelligent: when India became independent, Dr. Ambedkar, who drafted the Constitution of India, was a shudra, the last in the hierarchy of the four varnas, but as far as the law is concerned, there is no equal in his intelligence. He was a world renowned authority."

Former US President, Barrack Obama addressed the Indian Parliament in 2010 and referred to the Dalit leader Dr. Ambedkar as a great and respected human rights champion and the main author of the Indian Constitution. Ambedkar's political philosophy has given rise to a number of political parties, publications and labour unions active across India, especially in Maharashtra.

His promotion of Buddhism rejuvenated interest in Buddhist philosophy among various sections of the population in India. Mass conversion ceremonies have been organised by human rights activists in modern times, emulating Ambedkar's 1956 Nagpur ceremony. Some Indian Buddhists consider him to be a Bodhisattva, although he never claimed this himself. Outside India, during the late 1990s, some Hungarian Romani people drew parallels between their situation and the situation of Dalit people in India and inspired by Ambedkar, they began converting to Buddhism.

His promotion of Buddhism rejuvenated interest in Buddhist philosophy among various sections of the population in India. Mass conversion ceremonies have been organised by human rights activists in modern times, emulating Ambedkar's 1956 Nagpur ceremony.

He advised the public to press forward in this spirit: "My final words of advice to you are – be educated, agitate, stay organised and believe in yourself. With justice on our side, I don't see that we can lose our battle. Fighting is a pleasure for me. The fight is completely spiritual. There is nothing material or social in it. For us, this fight is not for money or power; it is a fight for freedom, it is a fight for the salvation of the human personality."

❑

3

Sakpal to Ambedkar

"I believe in a religion that teaches liberty, equality and fraternity."

–**Bhimrao Ambedkar**

God knows what kind of problems Bhimrao Sakpal overcame with the strength of his will and somehow reached school to study. But, he was not allowed to sit in the class. After a lot of struggle, when he got a place, it was at the back. During this period, whenever he felt thirsty, he was prevented from touching public water pitchers or even drinking water. There was a separate pitcher for him to drink from. This pot was not just different; it made children like him feel that they belonged to a caste which people used to humiliate by calling inferior.

He could not tolerate this difference in things like water. His first rebellion in childhood itself was based on the question of why there was a difference of high and low in children. However, he also had to suffer the consequences of rebellion. He was prevented from achieving anything that would have given him even a little bit of happiness. The process of prevention was already going on and it did not stop.

One of his Brahmin teachers, Mahadev, was very fond of him. It was on his request that Ambedkar removed Sakpal from his name and added Ambedkar, which was derived from the name of his village, 'Ambavade'.

Ambedkar achieved whatever he was prevented from achieving. He was prevented from reading books; he formed such a friendship with books that he became the first Law Minister of India. He held the oppressed in such a way that even today, he is alive in their hearts. He was prevented from going

Ambedkar achieved whatever he was prevented from achieving. He was prevented from reading books; he formed such a friendship with books that he became the first Law Minister of India. He held the oppressed in such a way that even today, he is alive in their hearts.

to the temple of God; he himself became the God of the hearts of the victims. He was stopped from thinking; he became a thinker himself. He was prevented by the laws of religion; he wrote the Constitution of the world's largest democracy. Such was Bhimrao Ambedkar, who had turned obstacles into a source of strength.

Steadfast in Challenges

Bhimrao was bright, intelligent and talented since childhood, but he had to face difficulties due to the thinking of the earlier society and being untouchable. Sometimes, due to this mentality, Bhimrao had to study outside the classroom, but apart from being talented, he had a passion for everything. He never accepted defeat or bowed down to challenges.

Bhimrao's father died when he was young. Due to the death of his father, the family became poor and faced a lot of difficulties. Ambedkar was fond of studies from the beginning. He had passed the matriculation examination in 1907 and in 1906, Bhimrao had a child marriage with Ramabai. At this time, Bhimrao was only 15 years old and Ramabai was 9 years old, but Bhimrao's passion for studies remained the same and he obtained a degree in Political Science and Economics from Bombay University in 1912.

❑

4

Nightmare Journey

"I have come into politics not to enjoy, but to give all my oppressed brothers their rights."

–Bhimrao Ambedkar

Bhimrao's family was originally resident of the Dapoli taluka located in Ratnagiri district of Bombay Presidency. After retiring from the army, his father went to Dapoli with his family to settle there again, but due to some reasons, he changed his mind. The family moved from Dapoli to Satara, where they lived until 1904.

Bhimrao has written one of his memoirs like this –

"According to my (Bhimrao) memory, the first incident is of 1901, when we lived in Satara. My mother had died. My father was working as a cashier in Koregaon of Khatav taluka in Satara district, where the Bombay government was digging ponds to provide employment to famine-stricken farmers. Thousands of people had died due to famine.

When my father went to Koregaon, he left me, my elder brother and my elder sister's two sons (sister had died) in the care of my aunt and some kind-hearted neighbours. My aunt was very good-hearted but could not help us much. She was a little short and had problems in her legs, due to which, she could not walk without support. Often, she had to be lifted and carried. I had sisters too. They were married and lived with their families at some distance.

When my father went to Koregaon, he left me, my elder brother and my elder sister's two sons (sister had died) in the care of my aunt and some kind-hearted neighbours. My aunt was very good-hearted, but could not help us much. She was a little short and had problems in her legs, due to which, she could not walk without support.

Cooking was a problem for us, especially because our aunt was unable to work due to physical disability. We four children used to go to school and also cook food. However, we could not make *chapatis,* so we had to make do with *pulao.* It was the easiest to make as it required nothing more than mixing rice and meat.

My father was a cashier, so it was not possible for him to come from Satara to see us. That is why he wrote a letter asking us to come to Koregaon during the summer vacations. We children got very excited just thinking about this because till then, none of us had seen a train.

Heavy preparations took place. New English-style kurtas, colourful and embellished caps, new shoes and new silk-bordered dhotis were purchased for the journey. My father had written and sent the complete details of the journey and said to write and tell when we left, so that he could send his peon to the railway station, who would take us to Koregaon. With this arrangement, I, my brother and my sister's son left for Satara. Our aunt was left to the neighbours who had promised to take care of her.

The railway station was ten miles away from our house, so a tonga was arranged to reach the station. We wore new clothes and left the house dancing with joy, but Aunty could not control her sadness at our departure and started crying loudly.

When we reached the station, my brother bought the tickets and gave me and my sister's son two annas each to spend on the way. We immediately splurged and first bought a bottle of lemon water. After some time, the train whistled and we boarded it quickly so that we would not be left behind. We had been told that we were to get down at Masur, which is the nearest station to Koregaon.

The train reached Masur at five in the evening and we got down with our luggage. Within a few minutes, everyone who got off the train went towards their destination. We four children were left on the platform. We were waiting for our father or his peon. Even after a long time, no one came. After an hour passed, the station master came up to us and checked our tickets and asked us why we were waiting. We told him that we had to go to Koregaon and were waiting for our father or his peon. We don't know how to reach Koregaon. We were wearing good clothes and even from our conversation, no one could guess that we were children of untouchables. That is why the station master was convinced that we were children of Brahmins. He felt quite sad about our troubles.

> *When we reached the station, my brother bought the tickets and gave me and my sister's son two annas each to spend on the way. We immediately splurged and first bought a bottle of lemon water. After some time, the train whistled and we boarded it quickly so that we would not be left behind.*

But, as usually happens among Hindus, the station master asked who we were. Without thinking anything, I immediately said that we are Mahars (Mahars are considered untouchable in Bombay Presidency). He was stunned. Suddenly, his facial expressions started changing. We could clearly see the feeling of disgust on his face. He immediately went towards his room and we remained standing there. Twenty or twenty-five minutes passed and the sun was about to set. We were surprised and troubled. Our happiness at the beginning of the journey had evaporated. We became sad. After about half an hour, the station master returned and asked us what we wanted to do. We said that if we could find a bullock-cart to rent, we would go to Koregaon and if it was not very far, we could also go on foot. There were many bullock-carts available for hire, but saying 'Mahar' to the station master was overheard by the cart drivers and no one was ready to take untouchables and become impure. We were ready to pay double the fare, but even the lure of money was not working.

But, as usually happens among Hindus, the station master asked who we were. Without thinking anything, I immediately said that we are Mahars (Mahars are considered untouchable in Bombay Presidency). He was stunned. Suddenly, his facial expressions started changing.

The station master who was talking on our behalf was not able to understand what to do. Suddenly, something came to his mind and he asked us, "Can you people drive the cart?" We immediately said, "Yes, we can drive it." Hearing this, he went to the cart drivers and told them that you will get double the fare and they will drive the cart themselves. The cart driver can himself walk alongside the cart. A cart driver agreed. He was getting double the fare and would also be saved from being defiled.

At about 6.30 pm, we got ready to leave but our concern was to leave the station only after being assured that we would reach Koregaon before dark. We asked the driver how far away was Koregaon and how long it will take to reach. He said that it would not take more than three hours. Believing what he said, we kept our luggage on the cart and after thanking the station master, sat on the cart. One of us took charge of the cart and we set off. The driver was walking alongside.

The station master who was talking on our behalf was not able to understand what to do. Suddenly, something came to his mind and he asked us, "Can you people drive the cart?" We immediately said, "Yes, we can drive it."

There was a river at some distance from the station. It was completely dry with small puddles of water here and there. The driver said that we should stop here and eat food, otherwise we will not get water anywhere on the way. We agreed. He asked for a part of the fare so that he could go to the neighbouring village and eat food. My brother gave him some money and he left, promising to come back soon. We were hungry. Aunty had the neighbours prepare some good food for us for the way, We opened the tiffin box and started eating.

Now, we needed water. One of us went towards a river water pit, but it smelt of dung and urine of cows and buffaloes. Without water, we appeased only part of our hunger and closed the tiffin and began to wait for the cart driver. He did not return for a long time. We were looking around for him.

Now, we needed water. One of us went towards a river water pit, but it smelt of dung and urine of cows and buffaloes. Without water, we appeased only part of our hunger and closed the tiffin and began to wait for the cart driver. He did not return for a long time. We were looking around for him.

Finally, he came and we moved ahead. We must have gone four-five miles when suddenly, the driver jumped into the cart and started driving. We were surprised that this was the same man who was not sitting in the cart for fear of becoming impure, but we could not muster the courage to ask him anything. We just wanted to reach Koregaon as soon as possible.

But soon darkness spread. The path was not visible. Neither man nor animal could be seen. We became scared. More than three hours had passed but there was no sign of Koregaon anywhere. Then, a fear arose in our minds that the driver was taking us to such a place where he would kill us and loot our belongings. We also had gold jewellery. We started asking him how far away Koregaon was. He kept saying, "It is not far, we will reach soon." It was ten o'clock at night. We started sobbing in fear and cursing the driver. He did not answer.

Suddenly, we saw a light burning at some distance. The cart driver said, "Look at that, it is the tax collector's light. We will stay there at night." We felt some relief. At last, in two hours, we reached the tax collector's hut.

It was situated on the other side at the foot of a hill. On reaching there, we found that a large number of bullock-carts were spending the night there. We were hungry and wanted to eat food, but there was no water. We asked the driver if we could get water anywhere. He warned us that the tax collector is a Hindu and if we

It was situated on the other side at the foot of a hill. On reaching there, we found that a large number of bullock-carts were spending the night there. We were hungry and wanted to eat food, but there was no water. We asked the driver if we could get water anywhere.

tell the truth that we are Mahars, we will not be able to get water. He said, "Say that you are Muslims and try your luck."

On his advice, I went to the tax collector's hut and asked if I could get some water. He asked, "Who are you?" I said that we are Muslims. I spoke to him in Urdu which I knew well, but the trick did not work. He said coldly, "Who has kept water here for you? There is water on the hill, go and get it from there." I returned to the cart with a sad face. When my brother heard what had happened, he said, let's go to sleep.

The oxen were untied and the cart was placed on the ground. We put a bed in the lower part of the cart and somehow lay down. I was thinking that we have enough food and are extremely hungry but without water, we have to sleep hungry and we could not get water because we are untouchable. While I was thinking this, a doubt arose in my brother's mind. He said that we should not sleep at the same time. Anything can happen. So, at one

The oxen were untied and the cart was placed on the ground. We put a bed in the lower part of the cart and somehow lay down. I was thinking that we have enough food and are extremely hungry but without water, we have to sleep hungry and we could not get water because we are untouchable.

time, two people will sleep and two will be awake. This is how our night passed at the foot of the hill.

At five in the morning, the cart driver came and said that we should leave for Koregaon. We refused and told him to leave at eight. We did not want to take any risk. He did not say anything. Finally, we left at eight o'clock and reached Koregaon at eleven. My father was surprised to see us. He said that he had not received any information about our arrival. We said that we had sent a letter. It turned out that my father's servant had received the letter but forgot to give it to him.

This incident has great significance in my life. I was nine years old at the time. The incident left an indelible impression on my mind. Even before this, I knew that I was an untouchable and that untouchables have to suffer some humiliations and discrimination. For example, in school, I could not sit with my peers. I had to sit alone in a corner. I also knew that I kept a sack for me to sit on and the school cleaner did not touch that sack because I am an untouchable. I used to take the sack home everyday and bring it back the next day.

I also knew that in school, when upper caste boys felt thirsty, they would ask the teacher and go to the tap and quench their thirst. But my case was different. I could not touch the tap. Therefore, it was necessary for a peon to be there after taking permission from the teacher. If there was no peon, I had to remain thirsty.

I also knew that in school, when upper caste boys felt thirsty, they would ask the teacher and go to the tap and quench their thirst. But my case was different. I could not touch the tap. Therefore, it was necessary for a peon to be there after taking permission from the teacher. If there was no peon, I had to remain thirsty.

My sister used to wash clothes at home too. It was not as if there were no washermen in Satara. It was also not as though we did not have money to pay them. Our sister had to wash clothes because no washerman would wash the clothes of untouchables. My elder sister also used to cut our hair because no barber would cut the hair of us untouchables.

"I knew all this, but that incident gave me a shock that I had never felt before. That is when I started thinking about untouchability. Before that incident, everything was normal for me, as it usually happens between upper caste Hindus and untouchables."

❑

5

Could Not Find a Place to Stay

Man and his religion should be chosen on the basis of morality through society. If religion is considered to be everything for man, then any other parameters will no longer have any value.

–Bhimrao Ambedkar

Bhimrao Ambedkar returned to India from the West in 1916. It was due to the Maharaja of Baroda that he went to America to pursue higher education. He studied at Columbia University in New York from 1913 to 1917.

He went to London in 1917. He enrolled in Masters at the School of Economics, University of London. In 1918, he had to leave his incomplete studies and return to India. Since the expenses of his education were borne by the Baroda State, he was forced to serve it. That is why he went straight to Baroda State after his return.

Five years of living in Europe and America erased his inner feeling that he was untouchable and that wherever an untouchable goes in India, he is a problem for himself and others. When he came out of the station, there was only one question in his mind: where to go, who will keep him? He was deeply troubled. He already knew that the Hindu hotels which were called Vishisht would not keep him. The only way to stay there was to lie, but he was not ready for this because he knew very well what the consequences would be if his lie was caught. They were predetermined. Some of his friends who had gone to America to study were from Baroda. Will they welcome him if he went to their place?

He could not reassure himself. They may feel embarrassed to invite an untouchable into their home. He stood there at the station for a while, feeling confused. Then it struck him to find out if there was any place in the camp. By then, all the passengers had left. He was the only one left. A few carriage drivers, who had not yet found a ride, were watching him and waiting for him. He called one of them and asked if there was any hotel near the camp. The driver told him that there was a Parsi inn and they take money and allow people to stay. His heart became happy after hearing that the Parsi people had arrangements for accommodation. Parsis are followers of the Zoroastrian religion. There is no place for untouchability in their religion, so he had no fear of being discriminated against for being untouchable. He kept his bag in the cart and asked the driver to take him to the Parsi inn.

It was a two-storey inn. An elderly Parsi and his family lived downstairs. They looked after it and made arrangements for food for those who came to stay. The carriage reached the inn. The Parsi caretaker took Ambedkar upstairs and showed him the room. Meanwhile, the driver brought his luggage and kept it there. Ambedkar gave him money and sent him away. He was happy that the problem of his accommodation had been solved. He was changing his clothes and wanted to rest for a while. Meanwhile, the caretaker came upstairs with a book. When he saw that Ambedkar was not wearing Sadri and dhoti, which is the typical Parsi way of dressing, he asked him in a sharp voice about his identity.

Ambedkar did not know that the inn was only for people of the Parsi community. He told the caretaker that he is a Hindu. The caretaker was surprised and said directly that Ambedkar could not stay there. He was stunned but remained completely calm. Then, the same question returned to haunt him: where to go? He controlled himself and said that even though he is a Hindu, he has no problem in staying here if the caretaker didn't have any. The caretaker replied, "How can you stay here? I have to enter the details of the people staying here in the register." Ambedkar could understand his problem. He said that he could keep some Parsi name to be recorded in the register. "What problem do you have with it if I don't? You will not lose anything; in fact, you will earn some money."

It was a two-storey inn. An elderly Parsi and his family lived downstairs. They looked after it and made arrangements for food for those who came to stay. The carriage reached the inn. The Parsi caretaker took Ambedkar upstairs and showed him the room.

Bhimrao was thinking that the caretaker was melting (convinced?). Anyway, he had not had any travellers for a long time and he did not want to miss the opportunity to earn a little. He agreed on the condition that Ambedkar would pay him Rs. 1.50 for accommodation and food and would enter a Parsi name in the register. The caretaker went downstairs and Ambedkar breathed a sigh of relief. The problem was solved, but Ah! until then, he did not know how momentary his happiness was. But, before we narrate the sad end of this inn story, let us tell you how Ambedkar lived there during this short interval.

Bhimrao was thinking that the caretaker was melting (convinced?). Anyway, he had not had any travellers for a long time and he did not want to miss the opportunity to earn a little. He agreed on the condition that Ambedkar would pay him Rs. 1.50 for accommodation and food and would enter a Parsi name in the register.

On the first floor of this inn, there was a small room and a bathroom attached to it which had a tap. Apart from that, there was a big hall. As long as Ambedkar lived there, the great hall was always full of junk like broken chairs and benches. Amidst all this, he remained there alone. The caretaker would bring a cup of tea in the morning, then he would bring his breakfast or something to eat again at 9.30 and for the third time, he would bring dinner at 8.30 pm. The caretaker would come only when it was absolutely necessary and he would avoid talking to Ambedkar on any of these occasions. Well, somehow these days passed.

He was appointed as an apprentice in the Accountant General Office by the Maharaja of Baroda. He would leave the inn at ten o'clock to go to the office and return at about eight at night and spent as much time as possible with friends in the company. The thought of returning to the inn to spend the night would scare him. He used to return there only because he had no other place under the sky. There was no other person to talk to in the large room on the upper floor. He was completely alone. The entire hall remained in complete darkness. There were no electric bulbs, not even oil lamps, which made it seem a little darker. The caretaker would bring a small lamp for his use, the light of which reached barely a few inches.

He was appointed as an apprentice in the Accountant General Office by the Maharaja of Baroda. He would leave the inn at ten o'clock to go to the office and return at about eight at night and spent as much time as possible with friends in the company.

He felt as though he had been punished. He yearned to talk to someone, but there was no one there and for this reason, he turned to books and kept reading them. He became so engrossed in his reading that he forgot his solitude, but the chirping sounds of the flying bats, for whom the hall was their home, would often draw his mind there. A shiver would run through him and he would once again remember what he was trying to forget – that he was in a strange situation in a strange place.

Many times, he would become very angry. Then, he would comfort himself by thinking that even though it was a jail, it was still a place to stay. It is better to have some place than no place. His situation was so bad that when his sister's son brought his remaining belongings from Bombay and saw his condition, he started crying so loudly that Ambedkar had to immediately send him back. In this condition, he lived as a Parsi in a Parsi inn.

He knew that this drama could not be kept up for long and that he would be recognised some day. So, he was trying to get a government bungalow, but the Prime Minister did not pay the attention that he needed to his petition. His petition kept moving from one officer to another. Before he could get a definite answer, that dreaded day arrived for him.

It was his 11th day in that inn. He finished breakfast, got ready and was about to leave the room for office. Actually, he was picking up the books that he had borrowed from the library for the night when he heard the sound of many people coming up the stairs. He thought that travellers

He knew that this drama could not be kept up for long and that he would be recognised some day. So, he was trying to get a government bungalow, but the Prime Minister did not pay the attention that he needed to his petition.

had come to stay and he got up to look at them. He saw dozens of angry, tall, strong Parsi men. All of them had sticks in their hands. They were coming towards his room. Ambedkar understood that they were not travellers and they soon proved it.

It was his 11th day in that inn. He finished breakfast, got ready and was about to leave the room for office. Actually, he was picking up the books that he had borrowed from the library for the night when he heard the sound of many people coming up the stairs.

All of them gathered in his room and bombarded him with questions. "Who are you? Why have you come here? You rogue! You have dirtied this Parsi inn!"

He stood silent and couldn't give any answer. He could not justify this lie. It was actually a hoax and the hoax was caught. He knew that if he continued this game in front of this fanatical Parsi crowd, it would have cost him his life. His silence saved him from reaching this fate. One of them asked him when he would vacate the room.

At that time, his life was at stake in exchange for the inn. There was a serious threat hidden in the question. Thinking that the minister would approve his request for a bungalow in a week, he broke his silence and requested them to let him stay for one more week, but the Parsis were not ready to listen to anything. They gave him a final warning that he should not be seen in the inn till (after) the evening. He had to leave. They told him to be prepared for serious consequences and left. Ambedkar couldn't think of anything. His heart sank. He kept muttering and wept bitterly. Ultimately, he was deprived of this precious place, yes, his place to live. It was no better than a prison, but it was still valuable to him.

After the Parsis left, he sat down and started thinking about some other way. He hoped that he would get a government bungalow soon and his problems would be solved. His problems were immediate and the solution could be found with his friends. He had no untouchable friends in Baroda, but from other castes. One was a Hindu, the other was a Christian. First, he went to his Hindu friend's house and told him the trouble that had befallen him. He was very good-hearted and a very close friend. He felt sad and angry. Then, he hinted that if Ambedkar came to his house, his servants would leave. Ambedkar understood his intention and did not ask him if he could stay in his house.

After the Parsis left, he sat down and started thinking about some other way. He hoped that he would get a government bungalow soon and his problems would be solved. His problems were immediate and the solution could be found with friends.

He did not find it appropriate to go to his Christian friend's place. Once, he had invited him to stay at his house. At that time, Ambedkar thought it best to stay in a Parsi inn. Actually, the reason for not going there was the difference in their habits. It was humiliating to go now. Therefore, he went to office, but had not given up the idea of going there. After talking to one of his friends, he again asked his (Indian Christian) friend if he could stay at his place. His friend replied that his wife was coming back to Baroda the next day and he would ask her and tell him.

He understood that this was a clever answer. The friend and his wife originally belonged to a Brahmin family. After becoming a Christian, the husband was generous but his wife was still a fanatic and would not allow an untouchable to stay in the house. This ray of hope was also extinguished. It was four o'clock in the evening when he left the house of his Indian Christian friend. Where to go? It was a huge question for him. He had to leave the inn, but there was no friend he could turn to. He had only one option and that was to return to Bombay.

He did not find it appropriate to go to his Christian friend's place. Once, he had invited him to stay at his house. At that time, Ambedkar thought it best to stay in a Parsi inn. Actually, the reason for not going there was the difference in their habits. It was humiliating to go now.

The train from Baroda to Bombay was at nine o'clock at night. He had to spend five hours but where to spend them? Should he go to the inn or a friend's place? He could not muster the courage to go back to the inn. He feared that the Parsis would gather again and attack him. He did not go to his friend' place. Even though his condition was very pitiable, he did not want to be an object of pity. He decided to spend time at the government park (garden), Kamathi Bagh, located on the edge of the city. He sat there distractedly and sorrowfully, thinking about what had happened to him. He thought about his parents and when he was a child and when they had bad days.

At eight o'clock at night, he came out of the garden and hired a car for the inn and collected his luggage. Neither the caretaker, nor he, said anything to each other. To some extent, the caretaker was considering himself responsible for Ambedkar's condition. Ambedkar paid his bill. The caretaker took it and went away silently.

At eight o'clock at night, he came out of the garden and hired a car for the inn and collected his luggage. Neither the caretaker, nor he, said anything to each other. To some extent, the caretaker was considering himself responsible for Ambedkar's condition. Ambedkar paid his bill. The caretaker took it and went away silently.

He had gone to Baroda with great expectations. He had rejected many opportunities for this job. It was wartime. There were many vacant posts in government educational institutions. He knew many influential people in London, but he did not take help from any of them. He thought that his first duty was to render his services to the Maharaja of Baroda who had arranged for his education. Here, he was forced to return to Bombay within eleven days.

That scene, in which dozens of Parsis are standing in front of him in an intimidating manner with sticks and he is standing in front of them begging for mercy with frightened eyes, could not fade away even after 18 years. It never happened that he remembered that day and tears did not come to his eyes. At that time, he realised that a man who is untouchable for Hindus is also untouchable for Parsis.

❑

6

Tonga–Accident

"Anyone's taste can be changed but poison cannot be converted into nectar."

–Bhimrao Ambedkar

This happened in 1929. The Bombay government formed a committee to investigate the issues of Dalits. Bhimrao was nominated a member of that committee. This committee had to visit every taluka and investigate atrocities, injustice and crimes. Therefore, the committee was divided. Ambedkar and another member were assigned to visit two districts of Khandesh. He and his companion parted ways after finishing the work.

Ambedkar's companion went to meet a Hindu saint and Ambedkar left to catch a train to Bombay. He got down at a village in Chalisgaon on the Dhulia line to investigate a scandal. Here, Hindus had started social boycott of the untouchables.

The untouchables of Chalisgaon came to meet him at the station and requested him to stay there for the night. His original plan was to investigate the boycott incident and leave straightaway, but they were very insistent and he agreed to stay there. He boarded a train to Dhulia to go to the village and investigate the incident and returned to Chalisgaon by the next train.

He saw that the untouchables (Dalits) were waiting for him at Chalisgaon station. He was garlanded with flowers. The houses of the Maharwada untouchables was two miles away from the station. One had to cross a river to get there, on which, a bridge (drain?) was built. Several horse-drawn carriages were available for hire at the station. Maharwada was at walking distance. He thought that they would go straight to Maharwada but there was no movement in that direction. He could not understand why he was being made to wait.

After waiting for about an hour, a tonga was brought to the platform and he sat in it. He and the carriage driver were the only two people in the carriage. The others went on foot through a nearby path. The tonga had barely travelled 200 yards when it almost collided with a vehicle. Ambedkar was very surprised because the driver, who must have been driving the horse carriage everyday, was driving like a novice. The accident was averted because the car driver turned the car back due to the loud shout of the policeman.

He saw that the untouchables (Dalits) were waiting for him at Chalisgaon station. He was garlanded with flowers. The houses of the Maharwada untouchables was two miles away from the station. One had to cross a river to get there, on which, a bridge (drain?) was built.

Anyway, somehow they came towards the bridge on the river. There were no walls on the sides of that bridge. A few stones were placed five to ten feet apart. The ground was also rocky. The drain built on the river was towards the town from where they were coming. They had to take a sharp turn from the bridge towards the road.

Near the stone on the drain, the horse, instead of going straight, turned sharply and jumped. The wheels of the cart got stuck in the stones on the edge in such a way that Bhimrao was jolted from it and fell on the rocky ground of the drain. The horse and cart fell straight from the drain into the river.

Bhimrao fell so hard that he became unconscious. Maharwada was just across the river. The people who had come to welcome him at the station had reached before him. Amidst crying children, men and women, he was picked up and taken to Maharwada. He had suffered many injuries. His leg was broken and he could not walk for several days. He couldn't understand how all this had happened. The tonga used to come and go on the same route everyday and the driver never made such a mistake.

Near the stone on the drain, the horse, instead of going straight, turned sharply and jumped. The wheels of the cart got stuck in the stones on the edge in such a way that Bhimrao was jolted from it and fell on the rocky ground of the drain. The horse and cart fell straight from the drain into the river.

On asking, he was told the truth. There was a delay at the station because no driver was ready to bring an untouchable in his cart. It was against his dignity. The Mahar people could not bear that Bhimrao would come to their home on foot. This was against their dignity. They found a middle path which was that the owner of the tonga would give it on rent but not drive it himself. The Mahars could drive it.

The Mahars thought that this would be fine, but they forgot that the safety of the ride was more important than dignity. If they had thought about it, they would have also considered if they could find a driver who could do the job safely. The truth was that none of them knew how to drive the cart because it was not their profession. They asked one of their own to drive it. One of them agreed thinking that there was nothing in it, but as soon as he made Bhimrao sit, he became nervous thinking about such a big responsibility and the cart went out of his control.

The Mahar people of Chalisgaon risked his life for their honour. At that time, he realised that a Hindu cart driver, even if he does the work of a horseman, has dignity. He can consider himself a person who is superior to an untouchable; it does not even matter that the untouchable is a government lawyer.

❑

7

Don't Touch Water

"We have to stand on our feet, fight for our rights. So, recognise your strength and power because power and prestige come only from struggle."

–Bhimrao Ambedkar

It happened in 1934. Some of Bhimrao's friends from the movement, who belonged to the Dalit community, asked him to go out with them. He agreed. It was decided that the plan should at least include the Buddhist caves of Verul. It was decided that first Bhimrao would go to Nasik and the rest would join him there. After going to Verul, they had to go to Aurangabad. Aurangabad was the

Muslim state of Hyderabad. It came under the area of His Highness, the Nizam of Hyderabad.

On the way to Aurangabad, they had to first pass through a town named Daulatabad. It was part of Hyderabad state. Daulatabad is a historical place and was once the capital of the famous Hindu king, Ramdev. The Daulatabad fort is an ancient historical building. Hence, no traveller misses the opportunity to see it. Similarly, the people of Bhimrao's party also included seeing the fort in their programme.

They hired some buses and passenger cars. They were about thirty people. They travelled from Nasik to Yeola. Yeola falls on the way to Aurangabad. Their visit was not announced. The plan was made quietly and knowingly. They did not want to create any uproar and wanted to avoid the troubles that an untouchable had to face in other parts of the country. They had also told their people the places where they had to stay. Due to this, no one came to meet them as they passed through many villages of the Nizam state.

It was definitely different in Daulatabad. Their people knew that they were coming. They were gathered at the entrance of the town and waiting for them. They asked them to get down and have tea and snacks and it was decided to see the Daulatabad fort. They did not agree to this proposal. They were very keen to drink tea, but wanted to see the Daulatabad fort properly before evening. So, they left for the fort and told their people that they would have tea on their return. They asked the driver to move and within a few minutes, everyone was at the gate of the fort.

This was the month of Ramadan (Ramzan), in which, Muslims fast. Just outside the gate, a small tank was filled to the brim with water. A stone path was also built on its side. During the journey, their faces, bodies and clothes were covered with dust. All of them felt like washing their hands and faces. Without thinking much, some members of the party stood on the rocky path and washed their hands and faces. After this, everyone went inside the fort through the gate. Armed soldiers were standing there. They opened a big gate and let them come straight inside.

It was definitely different in Daulatabad. Their people knew that they were coming. They were gathered at the entrance of the town and waiting for them. They asked them to get down and have tea and snacks and it was decided to see the Daulatabad fort. They did not agree to this proposal.

They asked the security soldiers about the way to go inside the fort. Meanwhile, an old Muslim came from behind, his white beard flying, shouting, "Thed (untouchable), you have polluted the water of the tank." Soon, many young and old Muslims who were nearby joined him and started abusing them. Thedas have gone mad. Thedas have forgotten their religion (what is their status). Thedas need to be taught a lesson. They adopted an intimidating attitude.

This was the month of Ramadan (Ramzan), in which, Muslims fast. Just outside the gate, a small tank was filled to the brim with water. A stone path was also built on its side. During the journey, their faces, bodies and clothes were covered with dust. All of them felt like washing their hands and faces.

Bhimrao and his companions told them that they have come from out of town and do not know the local rules. They started venting their anger on the local untouchable people, who by that time, had reached the gate. Why didn't you tell these people that these tanks cannot be used by untouchables? They started asking them these questions continuously. These poor people were not even there when the party had been near the tank. It was entirely their fault because they had not even asked anyone. The local untouchable people protested that they did not know.

However, the Muslim people were not ready to listen to them. They kept abusing them. They were abusing so badly that even they were unable to tolerate it. A riot-like situation had developed there and murder could have taken place, but they had to control themselves somehow. They did not want to create a criminal matter that would put an awkward end to their trip.

A Muslim youth from the crowd kept saying that everyone will have to tell his religion. This means that someone who is untouchable cannot take water from the tank. Bhimrao's patience ran out. He asked a little angrily, "Is this what your religion teaches you? Will you stop an untouchable from taking water if he becomes a Muslim?" These direct questions seemed to have some impact on the Muslims. They did not answer and stood silently.

Bhimrao's patience ran out. He asked a little angrily, "Is this what your religion teaches you? Will you stop an untouchable from taking water if he becomes a Muslim?" These direct questions seemed to have some impact on the Muslims. They did not answer and stood silently.

Turning towards the security guard, he again asked angrily, "Can we go inside this fort or not? Tell us and if we cannot go, we don't want to stay here." The security guard asked his name. Bhimrao wrote his name on a paper and gave it to him. The guard took the paper inside to the superintendent and then returned. They were told that they could enter the fort, but cannot touch water anywhere within the fort and an armed soldier was also sent with them to ensure that they would not violate that order.

In an earlier example we saw how an untouchable Hindu is also an untouchable for a Parsi; whereas, this example shows how an untouchable Hindu is an untouchable even for a Muslim.

Ambedkar, who had a childhood full of poverty, exclusion and stigma buried in a corner of his mind, had seen what kind of life millions of people like him were living in India. Only education can bring light in their life and soul. This will free them from the slavery which society, religion and philosophy have imposed in their veins.

Dalits were asked to accept this slavery as their destiny. Ambedkar wanted to break it. He was imagining a free man who would break the chain of gods and who would be religious, but not consider inequality as the value of life. Therefore, when he renounced Hinduism in

Ambedkar, who had a childhood full of poverty, exclusion and stigma buried in a corner of his mind, had seen what kind of life millions of people like him were living in India. Only education can bring light in their life and soul. This will free them from the slavery which society, religion and philosophy have imposed in their veins.

October 1956, he made himself and his followers take 22 vows.

These vows were related to disbelief in the Trinity of Hinduism, refutation of the incarnation theory, *Shraddh-tarpan*, abandonment of *Pind daan,* faith in the principles and teachings of the Buddha, non-participation in any ceremony performed by Brahmins, belief in the equality of human beings, following the Eightfold Path of the Buddha, kindness towards living beings, not stealing, not lying, not consuming alcohol, renouncing Hinduism based on inequality and adopting Buddhism. Ambedkar was a child of modernity, democracy and justice. He was also a lawyer by profession. He could not even imagine modernity, democracy and justice without giving equality to the dignity of man.

Related to belief in the equality of human beings, following the Eightfold Path of the Buddha, kindness towards living beings, not stealing, not lying, not consuming alcohol, renouncing Hinduism based on inequality and adopting Buddhism.

He fought for the equality of women in Indian society, both at home and outside. When he became the Law Minister in the government of Jawaharlal Nehru, he introduced the Hindu Code Bill to empower women, not only in the domestic world, but also economically and sexually. This bill was not allowed to pass. Ambedkar resigned.

8

Kalaram Temple Movement

"Although I was born a Hindu, I honestly assure you that I will not die as a Hindu."

–Bhimrao Ambedkar

Dr. Ambedkar struggled a lot to end untouchability. His Kalaram Temple Movement is considered very significant. The aim of this movement was not only to warn upper caste Hindus, but also to wake up the British.

This fight of Ambedkar was to provide rights to the Dalits and the exploited. The movement began on 2 March 1930 and lasted for five years.

Situated on the banks of the river Godavari, Nasik was considered the stronghold of Sanatani Hindus. Ambedkar's intention was to enter the Kalaram temple in the same Nasik, along with thousands of 'untouchables'. Dr.Ambedkar's biographer, Dhananjay Keer writes, "Ambedkar had courageously challenged the Brahmans of Maharashtra."

At that time, the British were ruling India. The Congress was fighting the British. On the other hand, Ambedkar was fighting against discrimination and exploitation of Dalits within the Hindu religion.

Ambedkar was challenging the privileges of the upper caste in Hinduism. Keer says, "Ambedkar's struggle was with the powerful Brahmins, who were not ready to give human rights to Dalits."

On 2 March 1930, a procession was taken out in Nasik. This city had never seen such a procession before. A meeting was organised under the chairmanship of Ambedkar, in which it was decided to take out the procession. The procession was to continue

On 2 March 1930, a procession was taken out in Nasik. This city had never seen such a procession before. A meeting was organised under the chairmanship of Ambedkar, in which it was decided to take out the procession. The procession was to continue for about one kilometre and about 15,000 people were involved in it.

for about one kilometre and about 15,000 people were involved in it.

This procession took place, raising slogans of Lord Rama. It reached near the temple. All the doors of the temple were closed, so the procession went to the banks of the Godavari river. A grand meeting was held there. It was decided to enter the temple the next day. The first agitating group consisted of 125 men and 25 women.

This movement continued for the entire next month. 9 April 1930 was the day of Ram Navami. An agreement had reached between Sanatani Hindus and the agitators led by Ambedkar. It was decided to include untouchables too in pulling Lord Rama's chariot. Ambedkar came to the temple with his supporters but the Sanatanis took the chariot away, before they could touch it. Ambedkar has narrated the entire episode in his letter written to the British governor of the Bombay province, Frederick Sykes.

His followers were pelted with stones. To prevent any stone from falling on Ambedkar, people had placed an umbrella over his head. People were injured. A young man had died in this incident. This is mentioned in a letter to the British Governor.

His followers were pelted with stones. To prevent any stone from falling on Ambedkar, people had placed an umbrella over his head. People were injured. A young man had died in this incident. This is mentioned in a letter to the British Governor.

Ambedkar's biographer, Dhananjay Keer has written, "After the *satyagraha,* the untouchables in Nasik had to face a lot of difficulties. Their children's schools were closed. Roads were closed. Goods from shops were no longer available to them. They were being pressured by Sanatani Hindus. Despite this, they continued the movement."

It was during the movement that Ambedkar had to go to London for the Round Table Conference. In his absence, Bhaurao Gaikwad continued the struggle. This struggle lasted for five years, although despite this, the untouchables were not allowed entry into the temple. After India got independence, the untouchables got entry into this temple.

But, he started this movement to bring the society which was suffering from casteism out of darkness and to send a message to the British. This struggle of Ambedkar was not limited to Nasik only. Earlier, he had also tried to enter the temple in Amravati. Such questions were being raised as to why a true devotee of Rama wanted an entry into the temple?

Ambedkar had answered this question in a meeting in Amravati. Ambedkar had said in his reply, "There are many types of prayer. One can have faith in God in both corporeal and incorporeal forms." However, he had to prove that "a temple does not become impure because of untouchable people or the glory of an idol does not diminish because of their touching it."

Ambedkar had said, "All classes have equal rights in Hindu religion. Here we cannot consider anyone untouchable. As much contribution has been made by untouchables like Valmiki and Ravidas to Hinduism as has been made by Brahmin Vashishtha, Kshatriya Krishna and Vaishya Tukaram."

Ambedkar had said, "All classes have equal rights in Hindu religion. Here we cannot consider anyone untouchable. As much contribution has been made by untouchables like Valmiki and Ravidas to Hinduism as has been made by Brahmin Vashishtha, Kshatriya Krishna and Vaishya Tukaram."

Non-violence was a major weapon in Ambedkar's movement. Ambedkar was not in favour of breaking any law. In view of this movement, the DM of Nasik had imposed prohibitory orders. Ambedkar had also requested the British Governor for entry into the temple but to no avail. Ambedkar had to postpone the entire movement.

In 1933, Mahatma Gandhi and Ambedkar met in Yerawada jail. Ambedkar had told Gandhi his opinion regarding entry into temples. He had told Gandhi that the oppressed classes would not gain their rights just by going to the temple. Social and cultural empowerment of this section is necessary. For this, education is most important. Ultimately, the caste system should also end; unless the caste system ends, their transformation cannot take place.

❑

9

Nothing is More Important than Education

"Nationalism can be justified only when, forgetting the difference of caste, race or colour between people, fraternity is given the highest place in it."

–Bhimrao Ambedkar

Bhimrao Ambedkar faced many difficulties from his early life till his last days, but he never let any of his problems come in the way of his education. Due to his hard work and enthusiasm, he got a scholarship to go to England for his further studies. Not only this, Babasaheb was very fond of reading books and had his own library, which housed a collection of more than 50,000 books. Also, when he was in London, he used to go to the library regularly.

Once, he was caught eating bread in the library during lunch time. The librarian warned him that his membership could be terminated. He also asked him to pay a fine. Ambedkar apologised to the librarian and told him that he did not have money to go to the cafeteria and eat. On hearing this, the librarian, who was Jewish, said to him, "Okay, from tomorrow, you come with me to the cafeteria and share my food with me." It is said that since then, Babasaheb used to give a lot of respect to Jews.

❑

10

Serious Towards Objective

"Unlike a drop of water which loses its identity by merging with the ocean, a man does not lose his identity in the society in which he lives."

–Bhimrao Ambedkar

When Ambedkar was studying at Columbia University in America, he used to often go to the library. He would reach the library in the morning before it opened and used to sit there till late night. Often, he used to stay in the library even when people went home after it closed.

Not only this, he even had to seek permission many times to sit in the library for a longer time. In one such situation, a library employee once told him that he had often seen him spending a long time there. He asked Ambedkar why he stayed with books all day long, instead of going out and having fun like other people. On this, Ambedkar replied to him in a very humble manner, “If I do the same as others are doing, then who will take care of my people, which is the sole purpose of my life?”

❑

11

Knowledge of Sanskrit

"People and their religions should be judged by social standards on the basis of social morality. If religion is considered necessary for the welfare of people, then no other standard will have any meaning."

-Bhimrao Ambedkar

Once, when a discussion was going on between Ambedkar and Lal Bahadur Shastri on some topic, both of them were conversing in Sanskrit. People were surprised at Dr. Ambedkar's hold on Sanskrit language, because since he had been born in an illiterate Dalit family, they were not ready to accept that he had mastered Sanskrit.

However, when Bhimrao Ambedkar was made the chairman of the Constitution Drafting Committee, he wanted to give an important status to Sanskrit, the mother of Indian languages, but he did not get the support of many other members of the Constituent Assembly, due to which, his dream of (towards) the development of Sanskrit remained unfulfilled.

❑

12

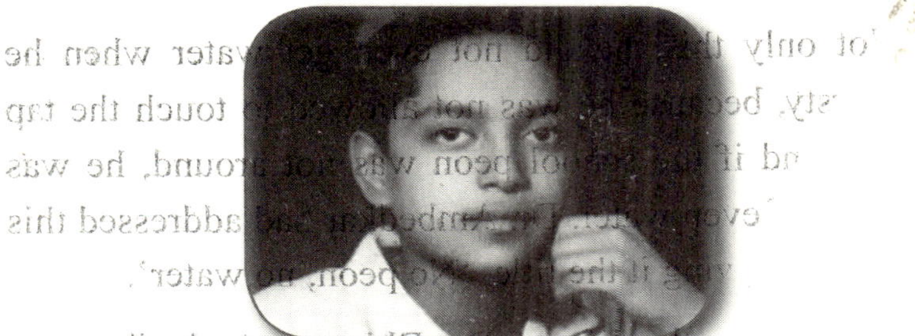

Deed is Bigger than Religion and Caste

"The religion that keeps one 'superior' and the other 'inferior' by birth is not religion. It is a conspiracy to keep one enslaved."

–Bhimrao Ambedkar

Dr. Ambedkar was born in a Dalit family, due to which, his entire life was spent in fighting for the rights of the exploited and destitute people. He writes about an incident from his childhood. In those days, Dalit people were looked down upon everywhere. In such a situation, when he used to go to school, he was not even allowed to sit and study with the other children.

Not only this, he did not even get water when he felt thirsty, because he was not allowed to touch the tap himself and if the school peon was not around, he was deprived of even water. Dr. Ambedkar had addressed this incident by giving it the title, 'No peon, no water'.

Thus, from the life of Dr. Bhimrao Ambedkar, we learn that a person should give importance to his deeds more than his caste and religion and if we follow the footsteps of Dr. Ambedkar, we will achieve success in every walk of life.

❑

13

Education for Social Change

"Caste is not a wall of bricks or a barbed wire that can stop Hindus from meeting each other. Caste is a concept, which is a state of mind."

–Bhimrao Ambedkar

Education is a primary medium for human, economic and social development which benefits both the individual and the society. It is a power and also the key to the well-being of the people. Dr. Ambedkar was very much aware of the importance of education in one's life. His life and struggle for education in early school life and even at higher levels including research, is a living

ucation shapes an individual and the
'e believed that both primary and
mportant for the common people
ressed classes. He said in the
ıcil, "We may give up the
on but we cannot give up our
gain the benefits of the

to provide more funds
e development of
education for all
people. In the
onation debate
y Assembly
dkar made
for the
lucation
first
ntry
e

collect from the people as special revenue."

Since change is a concept related to society, social change occurs only when the social structure, patterns of social relations, established social norms and social rules change. Technology, demography and ideology as well as changes in political life and economic policy (such as globalisation) bring about revolutionary changes in society. Cultural factors such as basic orientation in religion, morality and social outlook influence the direction and extent of social change.

Technological development impacts social change through introducing new methods of production by employing labour saving devices, faster transportation and communication systems and new reproductive methods. Electronic media, electronic devices, television, communication means and equipment, automobiles and construction technologies also bring changes in the social life of every individual.

With changes in the human practice of reproduction and advances in medical science, there are changes in population, family size, standard of living and intensity of inter-familial relationships. Thus, change leads to more and more education and education brings change.

With changes in the human practice of reproduction and advances in medical science, there are changes in population, family size, standard of living and intensity of inter-familial relationships. Thus, change leads to more and more education and education brings change.

There is no need to emphasise that education is a catalyst to bring social change in the society. The development of any society depends on the educational status of that society. Education is an agent or instrument of social change. It is seen as a major factor in the upliftment of the society. Its main function is the socialisation of youth and maintenance of social order. As opposed to this, the darkness of illiteracy always becomes a hindrance in the development and upliftment of the society. This darkness can be removed by the flame (torch) or light of education.

Education is an important factor for social change at various levels because it enables the formation of public opinion and the dissemination of knowledge for public welfare which arms the people against exploitation, superstition and establishes a new social order based on equality, justice and fraternity.

Education is an important factor for social change at various levels because it enables the formation of public opinion and the dissemination of knowledge for public welfare which arms the people against exploitation, superstition and establishes a new social order based on equality, justice and fraternity.

Dr. Ambedkar did not see education merely as a means of developing a child's personality or a source of earning livelihood; rather, he considered education as the most powerful agent to bring about desired changes in the society and considered it a prerequisite for organised efforts to start any social movement in the modern society.

Social Democracy

Dr. Ambedkar was one of the tallest figures of modern India, who freed a vast section of the Indian people from the infamous, inhuman, irreversible condition of divine slavery. He was a great social liberal. His vision was to create a new social order based on the principles of liberty, equality and fraternity. Thus, the ideas of liberty, equality and fraternity were the focus of his activities.

According to him, the concept of a 'just society' essentially reflects respect for the good life of its members and seeks to promote equality, in so far as it is consistent with its welfare ideals. A just society seeks to protect the lives of all its members, no matter how different they are. It allows for equal

The concept of a 'just society' essentially reflects respect for the good life of its members and seeks to promote equality, in so far as it is consistent with its welfare ideals. A just society seeks to protect the lives of all its members, no matter how different they are.

consideration, equal opportunity and equality before the law, where the interests of fair equality of opportunity and the well-being of the disadvantaged require differential standards of justice.

He wanted to establish an equitable social order and bring social justice for all through democracy. According to him, it was necessary to establish a government of the people, for the people and by the people to remove the social, economic, political and religious disabilities of the deprived classes. The ultimate aim of his life was to create 'real social democracy'.

In his concluding speech in the Constituent Assembly he said, "Political democracy cannot survive unless there is a basis for social democracy. What does social democracy mean? It means a way of life that recognises liberty, equality and fraternity, which must not be treated as separate objects in the Trinity. They form a union of trinity in the sense that to divorce one from the other is to defeat the purpose of democracy. Liberty cannot be separated from equality; equality cannot be separated from freedom, nor can liberty and equality be separated from fraternity."

It would also be appropriate to mention here that without education, the objective of social justice cannot be achieved, especially for Dalits and deprived sections. Therefore, Dr. Ambedkar was of the view that education is a powerful means to achieve social justice and without education, the attainment of social justice is only a dream.

> *It would also be appropriate to mention here that without education, the objective of social justice cannot be achieved, especially for Dalits and deprived sections. Therefore, Dr. Ambedkar was of the view that education is a powerful means to achieve social justice and without education, the attainment of social justice is only a dream.*

Realising the importance of education for the people of the depressed classes, Ambedkar believed that the more widespread the education, the greater the opportunities for the progress and betterment of the masses.

As a great educationist, he believed that education leads to overall development in one's life. Dr. Ambedkar expresses his belief in very strong words, "As I come from the lowest order of Hindu society, I know the value of education. The problem of the lower order is considered to be economic. This is a big mistake. The problem of raising the lower classes in India is not to feed them, clothe them and render them service of a high order, as is the ancient ideal of this country. The problem of the lower order is to remove from them the feeling of inferiority which has stunted their development and made them slaves of others and to create in them, a consciousness of the importance of their lives for themselves and the country, which has been brutally looted from them by the existing social system. This objective cannot be achieved except through the spread of higher education to all. In my opinion, this is the panacea for all our social problems." This is the reason Dr. Ambedkar made 'education' the first step of his clarion call of action, 'Educate, Agitate, Organise'.

As I come from the lowest order of Hindu society, I know the value of education. The problem of the lower order is considered to be economic. This is a big mistake. The problem of raising the lower classes in India is not to feed them, clothe them and render them service of a high order, as is the ancient ideal of this country.

Dr. Ambedkar, who was well aware of the issues of social inequality and injustice, got an opportunity to establish social justice in India when he was appointed Chairman of the Drafting Committee of the Constitution of India.

Here, Dr. Ambedkar was asked to include his ideas and ideals in the Constitution of the great nation. In the light of freedom in this great work, Dr. Ambedkar played a unique role in his capacity as Chairman of the Drafting Committee. He worked day and night to write the first Constitution of independent India, which included freedom, equality and justice. The theme of social change, social revolution and a charter of social justice running through the actions and documents of the Constituent Assembly.

Here, Dr. Ambedkar was asked to include his ideas and ideals in the Constitution of the great nation. In the light of freedom in this great work, Dr. Ambedkar played a unique role in his capacity as Chairman of the Drafting Committee.

The ultimate goal of the Constitution of India is to achieve social justice, through which a casteless, classless and egalitarian society may be able to translate into justice, equality, liberty and fraternity. The four fundamental pillars of the Indian Constitution, the conscience of the Indian Constitution, can be seen in the Preamble, along with Fundamental Rights and Directive Principles.

To correct the Indian society, which was subject to many injustices especially for the weaker sections, the provision of reservation or adequate representation for Dalits in government jobs, educational institutions, legislature, panchayats and municipalities was also included in the Indian Constitution.

The Constitution of India provides for protective discrimination in favour of the socially and educationally weaker sections for their upliftment, without disturbing the general concept of equality among the citizens of the country. Special provisions have been made in the Constitution for advancement and reservation.

The Constitution of India provides for protective discrimination in favour of the socially and educationally weaker sections for their upliftment, without disturbing the general concept of equality among the citizens of the country. Special provisions have been made in the Constitution for advancement and reservation.

Dr. Ambedkar designed these rights with the main objective of removing and eliminating inequalities and establishing an egalitarian society based on the feelings of equality, love and brotherhood. Dr. Ambedkar's idea of bringing positive social change in the Indian society through social justice is also reflected in Part IV of the Constitution of India, which is an 'innovative feature' of the Indian Constitution and promotes the idea of social and economic democracy in India.

Education is the means to achieve equality at all levels in a society, especially in India. Apart from achieving economic progress, education is a powerful tool in the process of overcoming inequalities and accelerating social change.

Ambedkar's philosophy of education is related to social liberation, which demands equal rights and educational opportunities for all; it stands for self-esteem and self-development and it also means a social revolution against the evils of slavery, untouchability, casteism, oppression etc. to remove social inequality in life.

Dr. Ambedkar particularly focused on removing inequality from the Indian society by providing Right to Equality and equal opportunity to the citizens of India, under Part III of the Constitution, which includes equal opportunities for education to all, irrespective of caste, creed, age, sex etc. The Constitution mandates the transformation of the traditional Indian social system from a society in which education was a privilege for small minorities into one where it could be made available to all people through various constitutional amendments.

Dr. Ambedkar particularly focused on removing inequality from the Indian society by providing right to equality and equal opportunity to the citizens of India, under Part III of the Constitution, which includes equal opportunities for education to all, irrespective of caste, creed, age, sex etc.

The basic thrust of Dr. Ambedkar's education philosophy is to inculcate the values of liberty, equality, fraternity, justice and moral character among citizens of all categories and it is quite evident through the various provisions of the Indian Constitution.

He struggled throughout his life for the rights of the oppressed classes in the society. He raised his voice against injustice, oppression, exploitation and atrocities.

His life, philosophy and mission were dedicated to all forms of social, economic and political justice and overall improvement of oppressed humanity. He was an advocate of all scientific and social activities which enhanced the cause of human progress and happiness.

Dr. Ambedkar stressed that legislation supported by social morality would not suffice to change the fortunes of the socially and educationally backward classes. Thus, he said, "Rights are not protected by law, but by the moral and social conscience of the society. If fundamental rights are opposed by the community, no law, no Parliament, no judiciary can guarantee them in the real sense of the word and it is education, which can inculcate these moral values in the students."

❑